About the Book

Penny didn't expect to go away for her vacation. She had no idea she would ever put her foot on foreign soil. Certainly she didn't plan to be a stowaway. But in this lively little book not only does one thing lead to another, it always leads to something more interesting.

This is a perfect adventure for young children because no one needs to worry very long. Penny is returned by a friendly sea captain with surprises of his own. Miss Clewes knows exactly how much fun there can be in an unexpected holiday.

THE HOLIDAY

by

Dorothy Clewes

illustrated by Sofia

Coward-McCann, Inc.　　　　　New York

For
SUSAN ELIZABETH
who lives
by the
sea

06209

© 1964 by Dorothy Clewes
Library of Congress Catalog Card Number:
64-17996

Manufactured in the United States of America

Contents

1

Everyone Is Going Away

"TOMORROW spring vacation starts," Penny said. "I don't go to school again for three whole weeks."

"It's nice that you'll have Jennifer to play with," her mother said. Jennifer lived next door. She was the same age as Penny and they went to the same school.

"Jennifer is going away," Penny said. She had been surprised and disappointed when Jennifer told her. Penny had made plans for all kinds of things they would do together.

7

"We're going camping," Jennifer said. "My mother and father and me and Rufus." Rufus was Jennifer's dog.

"You mean, you aren't going to stay in a house?" Penny asked.

"We're going to live in a tent," Jennifer said. "We're going to do our own shopping and cook our own food. It will be like one big, long picnic."

It sounded exciting and adventurous, but Penny's mother didn't think so.

"It *sounds* exciting," she said, "but I would rather sleep in my own bed and eat my meals sitting at a table. I don't like bees in my jam and flies swimming in my soup."

"It's going to be just like it was before Jennifer came," Penny said. The house next door would be empty, the windows would be closed tight and when she called through the fence no one would answer.

"There's Susan and Peter," her mother said. "They'll be glad to have you play with them."

Susan and Peter were twins. They had come in a big ship many miles over the sea from South Africa to live with their grandfather in the large house on the edge of town. Penny had asked a lot of questions about the ship because

8

she had never been on one. Susan had told her all about the cabin she and Peter had had to themselves. They had slept in bunks instead of beds — one little bed above another with a tiny stepladder reaching up to the top bunk, which had been Peter's. And there had been a little round window on one side of the cabin through which all they could see was water for days and days and days.

"Were you seasick?" Penny had asked, because grown-ups made such a fuss about going in even a little boat.

"Of course not," Peter said, "not even when it was rough. The Captain let us go on the bridge and we were allowed to look around the engine room. When I'm old enough I think I'll be a ship captain."

Penny had wanted to ask more about the bridge which was on a ship and the engines that pushed the ship through the water, but she was afraid Peter would laugh at her for not knowing.

"Susan and Peter are going away, too," Penny told her mother.

"We're going to the country," Susan had said, "to stay with an uncle we've never seen."

"He lives near a river," Peter had added. "He's promised to take me fishing."

"Well, what about Maxwell?" Penny's mother was as sorry as Penny that her friends were going away because she herself had been an only child too and she could remember that it wasn't much fun playing alone. Maxwell had been the first friend Penny had made. He lived on a farm a little way out of town and once Penny had gone to stay with him there. "Maybe this time he could come and stay with you," Penny's mother said. "I'll write to his mother and father tonight."

2

Maxwell's Father Says Yes and No

ALL the next day Penny spent planning what she would do when Maxwell came to stay. If her mother would give them an old sheet perhaps they could make a tent and live out in the garden. She didn't think her mother would let them cook their meals outside but it would be a picnic just the same. It would be almost as good as being in the country because the trees that had been bare all winter had suddenly burst into leaf. If they built the tent with its back to the house, it would be easy to imagine that they were really miles away from the town.

"Will there be a letter in the morning?" Penny asked her mother.

Her mother was just going to say Yes, I think so, when there was a loud knock on the front door.

"It's here now," Penny cried and ran to open the door. But instead of the postman, Maxwell's father stood there.

"The very one I wanted to see," he boomed.

"We were just talking about you. Come in," Penny's mother said. "I hope you're not going to tell us that Maxwell can't come to spend some of his vacation with Penny."

"Well, yes and no," Maxwell's father said.

Penny didn't see how it could be both. Either Maxwell could come or he couldn't.

"He can't come because he's going away," Maxwell's father said. "He has to go alone, too, because his mother and I can't get away. Farmers aren't like other people," he said to Penny's mother. "They can't pack their bags and catch the next train. The cows won't wait to be milked and they have to be fed and watered. The hens need their corn and the eggs have to be collected. The pigs have to be given their mash and their sties have to be cleaned out and filled with fresh straw. We never can take a vacation all together."

"I'm ashamed to say we never think about it like that,"
Penny's mother said. "We expect the milk to be on the step
when we open the door in the morning, and we take it for
granted there'll be bacon and eggs for breakfast."

"Well, that's the way it goes," Maxwell's father said. "It
wouldn't be natural if we stopped to think about everything. When your letter came this morning Maxwell said,

'Why can't Penny come with me?' We think it would be a good idea and we hope you do, too."

"Well, I really don't know what to say," Penny's mother said.

"Oh, say yes. Please, please say yes," Penny begged. Everyone was going away and suddenly there was a chance for her to go, too.

"Maxwell's going to stay with his grandparents at Seaport," Maxwell's father said, "so you wouldn't have to worry. Besides, he's old enough to take care of himself and Penny, too." Actually Maxwell was only two years older than Penny but he seemed more than that because helping on the farm had made him think about things in a very grown-up, sensible way.

"Oh, do say yes," Penny urged her mother. Going to the seashore would be a *real* vacation.

"It isn't what you mean by seashore," Maxwell's father explained. "It's what its name says: a seaport. You won't be able to swim but there's something going on all the time and there'll be plenty for you to watch."

"Isn't Seaport where the steamers leave to go across to France?" Penny's mother asked. "I remember going there once and I remember wishing I could go across the water on one of the boats to see just how different it was on the other side." She laughed. "I didn't go and I still haven't been, but one day we'll all go."

"But can I go — with Maxwell — now?" Grown-ups *talked* so much, Penny thought impatiently. All her mother had to say was yes.

"Not across to France," her mother said at last, "but to Seaport, perhaps. We'll have to see what your father says."

"I'll be driving them down," Maxwell's father said. "It only takes an hour and a half, and I'll go and get them when it's time for them to come back. We'll be leaving the day after tomorrow if Penny can be ready as soon as that."

Penny could have been ready that very minute. All she really needed was her coat and her pajamas and her toothbrush, but her mother, she knew, would insist on all sorts of preparations. Her hair would have to be washed, and her bag packed with a change of shoes in case she got her feet wet, a best dress in case she was taken out for dinner, and warm clothes in case it turned cold.

"The moment Penny's father comes home we'll telephone you," Penny's mother said.

3

Penny's Father Says Yes

PENNY'S father said yes, and what a lucky girl she was and called Maxwell's father to say thank you very much and Penny would be ready when they called for her.

Waiting for a birthday was hard enough, Penny thought, and waiting for Christmas was even harder, but waiting for a vacation to begin was the hardest of all. When she woke up the next morning there was a whole day and a night before it was time to go.

"The time will go faster if you don't think about it," Penny's mother said. "Put your coat on and we'll go shopping."

They shopped for a new toothbrush, a tube of toothpaste, a face cloth, and a pretty toilet bag to put them all in.

They bought new socks, a pair of sandals, two new hair ribbons, a cardigan sweater and a pleated skirt to go with it.

"It looks as if you've been buying your trousseau," her father said.

Later Penny's mother washed her hair and for once Penny didn't complain when the soap got in her eyes. She was thinking about the long ride to Seaport and what it would be like when they got there.

Then it was dinnertime and when Penny had helped to clear the table and dry the dishes her mother said, "Now it's time for you to pack your suitcase."

It was fun arranging all the new things, and even the old ones looked more interesting folded in tissue paper and placed neatly one on top of the other in the case, with the toilet bag tucked in at one side and the new shoes at the other.

"Now bath and bed and I'll bring you up a glass of milk," Penny's mother said.

"I don't feel sleepy," Penny said as her mother tucked her in and drew the curtains to shut out the light.

"Close your eyes and count up to ten," her mother said, and shut the bedroom door softly behind her.

"One — two — three —" Penny counted. "I wonder if we'll drive in the farm truck or in Maxwell's father's car?" In the truck you sat higher and could see over the hedges. In the car Penny had to sit up very straight to see out of the windshield at all. "Four — five — six — I wonder if the sun will be shining?" Penny didn't mind rain but when the sun shone everything else shone, too. "Seven — eight —"

"Eight o'clock. Time to get up. I thought you didn't feel sleepy. I thought you were going to stay awake all night." Her mother laughed, shaking her.

"Is it really today?" Penny was wide awake now, throwing back the bedclothes and jumping out of bed.

"It's today and the sun is shining. It's a real vacation morning."

This morning there was no need to say drink your milk, or eat your cornflakes. Penny had finished breakfast almost before anyone else had begun.

"Well, I'm not on vacation," her father said, "so I can't stay to see you off. Don't do anything I wouldn't do," he joked, "and if you get to France send me a postcard."

Penny walked with him to the garden gate and waved until he disappeared around the corner. When she turned back the farm truck was coming down the road.

4

The Road to Seaport

"I'M killing two birds with one stone," Maxwell's father said. "I have a piece of machinery to pick up from the factory close to Seaport."

Penny was glad that they were going in the truck. She sat between Maxwell and his father and she was high enough to look down into other cars that passed, as well as over garden walls and fences. At first they followed all the other traffic through the town, stopping at crossings for people to walk to the other side, and waiting at the traffic lights when they glowed red and moving on again when they changed to green.

At last they came to the end of the stores and the houses.

Suddenly they were in the country, passing fields and woods, running beside railways, crossing over bridges and running under them.

"Fifty-eight miles to Seaport," Maxwell read out from a signpost.

"Be there in just over an hour," Maxwell's father said, and put his foot down on the pedal that made the truck go faster.

"Does your grandmother live near the sea?" Penny asked Maxwell.

"Yes, right close to the harbor," Maxwell told her. "My grandfather is a Customs Officer and has to be near his work. From his back windows you can see ships coming and going all the time."

"To and from France," Penny said, remembering what her mother had said.

"Those are the steamers," Maxwell said. "Other boats come and go, too — from Holland and Germany and Denmark. If I weren't going to be a farmer I'd like to be a Customs Officer."

They came to a village and then another village, then a town and into the country again. All the time there were

more and more fields and more and more woods until suddenly they came to a river. The road ran beside it and every now and again it twisted away but it always came back again.

"It runs into the sea at Seaport," Maxwell told her. "When we get to the estuary we're nearly there."

Penny had never heard of an estuary.

"It's the tidal mouth of a large river," Maxwell said. "When the tide is high the river is full, as it is now. When the tide is out the river is just a stream running between muddy banks."

Now they came to a railway and when they had rattled over that the fields and the woods had gone. Stores lined the road again and in the distance, poking above the roof-tops and the chimneys, Penny could see a forest of thin, black, pointing spikes.

"That's the harbor," Maxwell told her, "and those are the derricks. They're a kind of crane for lifting goods out of a ship's hold."

"Shall we be able to see them doing it?" Penny asked.

Maxwell's father laughed. "You'll have a time getting Maxwell to do anything else. I think if he weren't going to be a farmer or a Customs Officer, he'd be a stevedore."

Penny had never heard that word before either.

"It's the name of the man who loads and unloads the ships," Maxwell's father told her, "and that's really hard work."

Ahead of them Penny could see funnels, some black, some white, some colored; some flying a tattered flag of smoke, and some looking as if they were just part of the scenery. In another moment Maxwell's father was turning to go through a large gateway onto the harbor itself.

5

Seaport

IT was like another world, Penny thought. Men in uniform were hurrying about, and porters, and rough, strong-looking men who must be the stevedores. Big buildings ringed the harbor and now the boats pressed up against the wall were as big as houses. They all had ladder-like planks running up to them and little boats hung from their sides. A few heads poked out of the round windows to watch the truck go by. Beyond the boats and as far as Penny could see was the blue, sparkling water, with wheeling, squealing sea gulls dipping and floating on the air, some even riding on the waves.

24

"And if you *could* see land, that would be France," Maxwell's father said.

The harbor wall was as broad as a road and they drove along it until they came to another gateway. This one led into a courtyard over which towered a block of apartment houses.

"That's Gran's apartment — right at the top." Maxwell pointed.

Penny had to tilt her head way back to see it. All the apartments had balconies with high, white-painted railings to make sure no one would fall over, but the top balcony looked the largest. Penny could see chairs set out on it and as she stared a tiny figure came to the railing and waved to them.

Maxwell and his father waved back and Maxwell cupped his hands around his mouth and shouted, "Hi! We're here."

Penny wondered how they were going to climb the many stairs there must be to take them up so high. But inside the hall Maxwell's father pressed a button and an elevator door slid open.

"I bet you thought we had to walk," Maxwell laughed,

as the elevator whisked them up. "Wait until you come down in it, it's like flying."

The tiny figure that had waved to them from the balcony was waiting for them as the elevator door slid open. She didn't look so small now, but plump and jolly, and as glad to welcome Penny as Maxwell.

"We'd been saying it was a shame there are no boys and girls in the house. Now you'll have a fine time together. Maxwell knows the harbor and a lot of people working on it. He'll show you everything."

Maxwell's grandfather came in then, looking very smart in a uniform that was like a ship's officer's if you hadn't known from the gold braid and the lettering on his jacket that he belonged to the Customs Department. Penny hadn't known what his job meant until Maxwell had explained that he was a kind of policeman.

"People try to smuggle things over from other countries," he told her, "some things that are cheaper there than they are here — watches from Switzerland, silk from Italy, wine from France. If they declare what they've brought back with them they're often allowed to keep it, but if they say they haven't anything and then some of those

things are found in their suitcases, they have to pay duty or give them up."

Penny didn't think that sounded fair. "Couldn't you even bring back a present?" she asked him, because this was something her aunts and uncles often did. One had brought her a doll from Austria that danced to a little tune when you wound her up, and the best dress in her suitcase had been brought for her by another aunt from France.

"They're pretty nice if you declare it," Maxwell said. "But if they allowed everything through that wouldn't be fair to storekeepers on this side. They have to pay duty, you know. The same thing happens in other countries when visitors take presents back from England," he assured Penny. "But some countries do set a fixed amount duty-free and as long as you don't take in more than that it's all right."

Maxwell thought this was a good idea and that it was too bad English customs didn't have the same rule. Maybe then people wouldn't be tempted to try to smuggle things through.

Certainly Maxwell's grandfather didn't look like the

kind of man who would take a present away from you at the end of a vacation, Penny thought. In fact, at this moment, he was giving them one.

"Here's five shillings for each of you," he said, diving his hand into his pocket. "It won't buy as much as it did when I was your age but I guess you'll know what to do with it."

They all had lunch and when Maxwell's father got up to go his grandfather got up, too. "The last cross-channel steamer's gone for today," he told Maxwell, "but you'll be able to take Penny to see the afternoon boat come in."

"Be careful what you do," Maxwell's father said, "and don't get into any mischief."

6

The Reine de France

PENNY saw the boat before Maxwell did — at least she saw the thin, black, smudgy line of smoke on the horizon.

"Yes, that's it," Maxwell agreed. "It's much farther away than it looks, though. There'll be time to show you around and then we'll come back."

They went to look at the railway lines which carried the trains that brought the passengers in from all parts of the country. A train was waiting at the platform, empty, but in the dining cars, tables were set and shaded lamps glowed among the china and silver.

"It's the boat train," Maxwell told Penny. "When the

passengers have been through Customs they'll pile in to be taken up to London, except those who have cars waiting, or cars with them. It's a car ferry as well as a passenger ferry. That's what makes it fun to watch."

They went to look at the parking lot then. It was filling up already, cars driven by chauffeurs, cars driven by passengers' friends or relations. There was a garage, too, with gas pumps and smart young men in white overalls filling cars with oil and water and gas so that time wouldn't be lost on the other side.

"One of the men here is a friend of mine," Maxwell said. He looked around, but his friend didn't seem to be there, so they went back to see if the boat had come any closer. It seemed just as far away as ever except that now it was a real shape under its plume of smoke.

"It's so small," Penny marveled. "It's like a toy."

"That's only because it's so far away. It's getting bigger all the time." Maxwell said. "Look, now you can just see the bridge."

Penny peered but she couldn't see anything that looked the least bit like a bridge.

"It's not like a bridge over a river," Maxwell told her.

"It's a kind of covered platform in the middle of the ship where the Captain has a clear view all around. It's the part that sticks out above the forrard deck. And 'forrard' is boat language for forward," he added.

She had been right to think it was a different world, Penny decided, if words you knew suddenly meant something else.

"Steps are gangways, and a knot isn't a tangle in a piece of string. It's a sea mile." Maxwell had known it all for so long that it hadn't seemed strange to him until now, and he began to think of other words. "A log isn't a piece of wood, but a book where a record of the trip is kept. Portside is the left-hand side of a ship and starboard is the right-hand side. And hatch doesn't have anything to do with eggs. It's an opening in the deck where the cargo is kept."

"And where you sleep isn't a bed, it's a bunk," Penny said, remembering what Susan and Peter had told her. "And you don't go to bed in a room but in a cabin, and you don't look out of windows but out of portholes."

"That's right," Maxwell said. Penny was always surprising him by knowing more than he thought she did.

"Susan and Peter told me," she said. "They lived on a

32

ship for days and days when they came from South Africa."

"I've been on a ship but I've never sailed in one," Maxwell said. "But when I do I'll know my way around."

A deep, trembly blast of sound floated on the breeze toward them, and then another and another. It echoed around the harbor and everyone turned around to see where it came from.

"She wants you to know she's coming," Maxwell said. "My grandfather says that's why they call a boat a 'she' — because they want a lot of attention."

Penny didn't know about that, but the steamer looked so beautiful gliding smoothly through the blue water that surely no one would want to look at anything else.

The steamer was so close now that Penny could see people walking around on the decks, and sailors leaning over the side waiting for the moment when she would slide into port: Seaport.

"All hands on deck," Maxwell said. "They don't waste any time. The moment the boat docks they're ready to disembark passengers and unload."

"I'm home. I'm home," boomed the steamer.

Nearer and nearer she crept. Now belowdecks sailors

had pushed away part of the boat rails and, peering into the dark, open hole, Penny could see automobiles and motorbikes, their engines throbbing, waiting only for the boat to be moored and for the wide gangplank to be pushed across the narrowing gap that separated them from the quayside.

"It's like a floating garage," she said.

"Stand back now," a porter cautioned them.

Penny had been so busy watching the boat come in that she hadn't noticed that the quayside, which had been almost empty a few moments ago, was now bustling with porters and stevedores and gold-braided officers. Friends and relations of the passengers had begun to gather closer, too, and some had already caught sight of those they had come to meet and were waving and exchanging shouted greetings.

The boat nudged gently up to the quayside and as if that were a signal a rope came snaking over the dividing strip of water. Someone caught it and slipped it over one of the thick round posts sprouting up all along the quay that Penny had thought were stools to sit on.

"They're bollards," Maxwell informed her. "Now she's tied up until she sets off again tomorrow."

Reine de France was painted in large black lettering on the side of the boat. Penny knew that France was the country the steamer had come from but the other two words looked strange. She couldn't even pronounce them.

"*Reine de France.*" The way Maxwell said it it sounded like "rain." "It's French and means 'Queen of France.' "

"Can we come tomorrow and see her go?" Penny asked. It would be like seeing a friend off because once anything had a name it became special.

"All right," Maxwell said, "but we'll have to be here early. She leaves just after nine."

7

Au Revoir

PENNY and Maxwell were down on the quayside
long before nine o'clock next morning, but even so
cars were being driven across the gangplank and into the
gaping side of the *Reine de France.* Some passengers were
already on deck arranging deck chairs in the best places and
settling themselves for the trip across. A thin drift of smoke
curled out of the funnel and twisted away on the breeze
as if there was all the time in the world before she had to
set out to sea.

"Well, if it isn't Maxwell!"

The deep, cheery voice came from the open window of a car farther down the waiting line of cars. Maxwell spun around to see who it was and at once recognized the young man behind the wheel.

"I looked for you at the garage yesterday, Tom," Maxwell said, running over to him, "but I couldn't see you."

"I imagine I was with the boss," Tom said. "He's making a trip to the other side and there was a lot to arrange. I'm taking the car on for him while he gets himself a deck chair in the sun. I suppose you're down here on vacation again?"

"A friend came with me this time," Maxwell said, as Penny joined them. "I'm showing her around. We were just wondering what it was like in there."

"Come and see for yourselves," Tom said. He put his hand over the back of the driver's seat and opened the door behind him.

"Do you mean it?" Maxwell hesitated. The car was a Panther. He had never been as close to one as this. To be asked now to ride in one — even if it was only across the gangplank and into the ship's parking space — wasn't to be missed for anything. He scrambled in and Penny jumped in after him.

"Have you ever been across?" Maxwell asked the young man.

"More times than I can count," Tom said. "A day like this is perfect: blue sky, sunshine and just enough breeze to make the sea interesting."

"What is it like on the other side?" Penny asked him.

Tom scratched his head. "Oh, I don't know. The same as here, but different, if you see what I mean."

Penny didn't see what he meant. It couldn't be the same because it was France, and if it was different someone who had been there so many times ought to know how different it was.

At that moment the car in front began to move and the young man started the engine of the Panther. Maxwell bounced up and down on the back seat. After the firm leather covering of the truck seat this was like sitting in an armchair. Penny, sitting in the other corner, had found a little drawer that pulled out of the end of the arm to make an ashtray, and in front of her — on the back of the front seat — a little flap came down to make a table. You could have a picnic while you traveled, Penny thought. It was a real little room on wheels.

Now it was their turn to bump over the gangplank. Looking through the window and down, Penny could see the narrow strip of water before they jolted off the plank and into the dark inside of the ship.

It was just like a parking lot. Cars were drawn up in neat rows on each side of a wide lane. The Panther followed closely behind the car in front and slid into place beside it.

"That's it, I'm afraid," Tom said. "We have to go up on deck to get off. Anyway, I have to have a word with the boss."

He took the little ticket that the man in charge handed him and led the way through the parked cars to where a stairway climbed up into sunshine again.

Penny stood on the scrubbed white boards and gazed down onto the quay where she had been standing only a moment before. Now she could imagine she was a passenger. She ran over to an empty deck chair to see what it felt like sitting close up to the edge, feet resting on the white rail in front of her.

"Is this your first time on a boat?"

Penny had thought she was alone but now she saw that a lady was sitting in the deck chair next to her. Penny was

40

only pretending to be a passenger but sometimes grown-ups didn't understand, and so she nodded her head.

"I well remember my first trip," the lady said. "I was about your age. When I got to the other side I was surprised that I couldn't understand what was said to me. What was even more surprising, they couldn't understand me. It was a good thing my parents were with me."

Boat language had been a kind of game but it sounded as if a foreign language was something very serious. Perhaps that was what the man from the garage had meant, Penny thought.

"Can you speak French now?" Penny asked the lady.

"*Oui*," the lady said. "That's French for yes," she explained. "Now you can say that you know one word."

"I know two," Penny said. "*Reine* is French for queen. That's the name of this boat."

"Well, I never," the lady exclaimed. "Imagine a little girl like you speaking French. Nowadays boys and girls know everything."

"I don't know the word for no," Penny said, because she was thinking that if she went to France that would be the word she would probably use more than any other.

42

"*Non*," the lady said. "It looks the same as our English no only it has an 'n' on the end which you don't sound when you say it. You're going to pick the language up in no time at all, I can see that, and then you'll feel as at home over there as you do here. Are you going to stay long?"

"*Non*," Penny said, and tried to imitate the sound the lady had made.

"Never mind," the lady said. "Perhaps when you're a little older you'll be able to go and live with a French family. I know lots of boys and girls who do that and it's the best way of all to learn."

Penny, who thought she would rather live in her own home, said, "Maybe a little French girl could come and live with me and learn English."

"Whichever way it is," the lady said, "it would be a splendid thing for both of you."

Behind the chair Maxwell's voice said, "There you are! I've been hunting all over for you. She's ready to sail."

Penny was glad to stop pretending. "I have to go now," she said to the lady.

"*Au revoir* then," the lady said. "You must come and talk to me again."

"What's *au revoir*?" Penny asked Maxwell, as they ran back to the little stairway that led down to the lower deck and the parked cars.

"Good-bye," Maxwell said, "and that's what we'll be saying to Seaport if we don't get a move on."

But the little stairway had gone. The parking space they gazed down into was full and the wide opening where the gangplank had spanned the narrow gap of water was now closed by the boat rail. Maxwell spun around and ran back the way they had come, Penny at his heels. They pushed through the deck chairs to the side of the boat to gaze down on the quayside, but that had gone, too. Between them and Seaport gaped a fast-widening stretch of water.

"Good-bye," boomed the ship's siren right above their heads. "Good-bye. Good-bye."

8

Stowaways

"WE'RE on our way to France," Penny said, and now it seemed exciting in quite a different way, an alarming way. And it was all her fault. If she hadn't sat down on the empty deck chair and pretended to be a passenger Maxwell wouldn't have lost her.

"It's as much my fault as yours," Maxwell said. "I knew we shouldn't have come on board in the first place, but I wanted to ride in the Panther and I wanted to see what it was like where they parked the cars."

It was really Tom's fault but he was a friend of Maxwell's and Penny didn't like to blame him. In any case he had only suggested it as a joy ride. He hadn't expected them to stay on board.

"What will we do?" Penny asked. She wasn't really frightened because she was sure Maxwell would know.

Maxwell had been really alarmed when he saw what had happened, but now it was beginning to dawn on him that it wasn't so terrible after all. "Well, she only goes there and back," he said. "All we have to do is stay on board."

Maxwell was right, of course, Penny realized with relief. And all at once she knew she didn't have to pretend any more; now she was a real passenger. She went to sit on the slatted seat which ran around the side of the boat and looked back at Seaport. She could hardly see it any more, but oddly enough, although it was so far away it seemed to have become suddenly much bigger. Now she could see tall white cliffs with stretches of sandy beach below them with the lacy edge of the sea rolling over it. There was a lighthouse, too, and behind and as far as she could see were green hills with little white houses dotted over them. And the edge of land had become the shape of part of the map in her school geography book.

46

"If we were in an airplane we'd be able to see even more," Maxwell said. "Then it would look like all of the map."

They watched until it disappeared completely and all they could see was a thin dark line dividing the sea from the sky.

"That's the horizon," Maxwell said. "Come on, there's nothing more to see now until we get nearer to the other side. Let's explore."

Lots of other boys and girls were chasing around so that no one thought it odd that Penny and Maxwell should be running around, too. Maxwell led the way forrard until they stood in the prow of the boat. The salt wind whipped the color into their cheeks and sent Penny's hair streaming out behind her. Now the deck dipped and rose under their feet as the boat creasted the waves and slid down into the little troughs they left behind them. This must be what the young man from the garage had meant when he said there was enough breeze to make the sea interesting. Interesting and fun, Penny thought, trying to keep her balance when the deck went up when she was expecting it to go down and down when she was expecting it to go up.

They climbed a little stairway to the top deck and had a closer look at the lifeboats. They couldn't see inside them because they were closely covered over with a waterproof jacket to keep the rain out. When they got down again onto the deck below everyone seemed to be moving to an even lower deck and Penny and Maxwell followed them.

After the bright sunshine outside they seemed to be going down into a black cavern, but a glorious smell of food tickled their noses and led them on.

"It's the dining room." Maxwell hadn't thought about what they would do when lunchtime came and now he realized he felt very hungry indeed. He put his hand into his pocket and took out the money his grandfather had given him. He hadn't expected he would have to spend it on food. Perhaps if they didn't each much —

"Well, if it isn't my little friend. Don't tell me you're traveling alone?"

It was the deck-chair lady. She was sitting at the table beside which Penny was standing.

"I'm traveling with my friend," Penny said, pulling at Maxwell's sleeve.

48

"Well now, if you're on your own and I'm on my own, why don't we lunch together?" the deck-chair lady said.

Maxwell hesitated. Grown-ups ate expensive things and if she ordered the same for them his money would soon disappear, and Penny's, too. He had been thinking that they could have a sandwich and a glass of lemonade.

"You'll be my guests, of course," the lady said, as if she had read Maxwell's thoughts.

"Roast chicken. I think that sounds nice, don't you?" she said, reading from a menu as large as a book. "And fried potatoes and green peas."

Penny thought it sounded like Christmas dinner and she wouldn't have been surprised if the lady had added, "and Christmas pudding." She did, almost, but instead of Christmas pudding she was saying, "And ice cream pudding."

Maxwell couldn't imagine what an ice cream pudding was like and hoped it wasn't rice pudding that had been put in the refrigerator to get cold.

Glasses of orange juice came with the roast chicken and baby sausages and delicious curls of crisp bacon. One half of Penny wanted to make it last forever and the other half couldn't wait for the ice cream pudding. And when that

49

did come it really looked at first as if it was just a very ordinary pudding — until the waiter cut into it. Underneath the cream-colored vanilla layer there was a green layer, and then a chocolate layer, and then a strawberry layer, and all of it was stuffed with tiny pieces of fruit. When she was grown-up and could do what she liked she would have it every day, Penny decided.

"How very exciting to be making the trip on your own," the lady said. "Tell me, where are you going?"

"To France," Penny said.

"But to what part of France?" the lady asked.

"Where the boat docks," Maxwell said.

The lady nodded. "Ah, now I'm beginning to understand. Your father has something to do with the shipping line."

"My grandfather is a Customs Officer." Maxwell wished the lady would stop asking questions. He thought he had managed very well so far to answer truthfully without making her suspicious, but he didn't know how long he could keep it up.

"We must keep together then," the lady said. "If I'm

with you maybe I'll be allowed the few presents I'm taking to my nephews and nieces."

"It's best to declare them," Maxwell said. "If you pretend and then you're found out they can be really tough." Suddenly as he spoke the words he realized that was exactly what he and Penny were doing — pretending to be something they weren't. He felt his cheeks begin to burn.

"How guilty you look all of a sudden," the lady said. "I do believe you're hiding something."

"No, he isn't." Penny rushed to defend him, though she couldn't imagine why Maxwell was looking so uncomfortable. "The only present we've got with us is five shillings Maxwell's grandfather gave each of us this morning."

"But I thought you said your grandfather lived in France, that you were on your way to visit him?"

Maxwell hadn't said anything of the sort but he knew that was the impression he had given. Now he didn't know what to say and before he could think of anything the lady said, "And if you mean your grandfather is an English Customs Officer he should know that English money will be no use to you in France. Over there you can only buy things with francs."

It was all much more different than Penny had realized, if the language was different and the money was different, too. Perhaps the people were different, and if they were —

"You know, I do believe you're stowaways," the lady said.

Maxwell still couldn't think of anything to say but it didn't matter any more because the truth was written on his face now for anyone to read.

"I'm going to have to speak to the Captain," the lady said. "I don't want to give you away, but I wouldn't be your friend if I didn't. I hope you understand that. Come along, we'd better go and see him now."

9

France

"STOWAWAYS!" The Captain glared down at them, eyes unsmiling under dark, shaggy eyebrows. "This is a very serious offense, do you know that?"

Maxwell nodded. They would probably be fined and he wondered if the money his grandfather had given them would be enough.

"Do I clap you in irons or string you from the yardarm?" The gold braid glittered on the Captain's arms and the gold buttons blazed on his chest.

He was talking boat language. Penny could recognize it now, and although she didn't know what it meant it was very clear from the look on the Captain's face that it was something very unpleasant, some kind of punishment.

"But it was an accident," she said quickly. "We didn't mean to be stowaways."

"That's what they all say, when they're caught," the Captain said.

"But it's true," Penny insisted. "I was pretending to be a passenger and by the time Maxwell found me the boat was on its way to France."

"Maxwell?" For a moment the Captain looked less fierce. "That's an unusual name. I only know of one other Maxwell and he's the grandson of a Customs Officer friend of mine."

"My grandfather *is* a Customs Officer," Maxwell said.

"Well, well." The Captain stroked the little pointed beard that grew on his chin. "And does he know you've stowed away?"

Maxwell shook his head. There hadn't been time to think of anything but what they were going to do and now he was remembering what a long time they had been away.

"It's past lunchtime," the Captain said. "Don't you think your grandparents are worrying about you?"

"Maybe you could send a message by radio," Maxwell suggested.

"So, now we're the *Queen Mary!*" Penny thought the Captain was going to explode and then to her surprise he burst out laughing. "You're my friend's grandson, all right," he said, and to Penny, "You stowed away with the right one, there's no mistake about that."

Penny couldn't imagine how the Captain was going to send a message to Maxwell's grandparents across all that long stretch of water so that they would be able to hear him. But he reached out his hand and lifted up what looked like an ordinary telephone and in a few moments he was talking direct to Maxwell's grandfather. There was no mistaking the voice. It came out of the instrument so clearly that both Penny and Maxwell could hear it, too — at first surprised, and then worried, and then relieved.

"I promise I won't let them out of my sight and that they'll be back on the afternoon boat," the Captain was saying. "Don't be too hard on them when they get home. It's something I always wanted to do when I was their age." And now, surprisingly, an eye under the bushy eyebrows winked at them.

The rest of what was said was suddenly drowned in the deep-throated boom of the ship's siren.

"We're there. We're there." And again, "We're there. We're there."

"If I'm not to let you out of my sight you'd better come with me to the bridge," the Captain said.

After all the bridge was just a room. But it was a room high above the decks with windows all around. Penny could see the long, smooth pathway they had made in the water behind them as well as the way ahead — a bustling quayside just like the one they had left behind, only in some odd way, slightly different.

"Slow," the Captain said to the man at the wheel.

"Slow it is," the helmsman repeated and moved the heavy lever in front of him so that a bell rang sharply.

The hum of the engines dropped to a quiet throb.

"Dead slow," the Captain ordered.

"Dead slow," the man at the wheel repeated. Again he moved the lever and again the bell rang.

Now the voice of the engine was a whisper and the boat was still, except for a gentle quiver. To Penny it seemed as if the boat was the quayside, and that the cranes and the porters and the stevedores and the crowd of people waiting there were moving toward them instead of the boat moving toward the quayside. She looked down on the waving, shouting mass of people, and it was just like looking down on the crowd of people they had left behind on the other side, except she couldn't understand what they were shouting.

"*Allo, Madeleine! Allo, Pierre et Jean!*"

Their clothes looked different, too, Penny decided. Not very different, but enough for you to know they weren't English clothes. But the people inside them looked the same, except they waved their hands around a lot when they talked.

"Finish with engines," the Captain ordered.

"Finish with engines," repeated the man at the wheel so that there wouldn't be a mistake. And now when the lever moved and the bell rang, the quivering whisper of the engines died away altogether and the boat was as still as a house.

They had arrived.

They were in France.

10

The Same – Only Different

PENNY sat on the deck chair and rested her feet on the white rail in front of her. She wasn't a stowaway any more but a passenger who had been across to France and was now on her way home.

"Won't they be surprised at home when they get the postcards?" Penny said. When her father had said, "If you get to France send me a postcard," he had only meant it as a joke. He certainly hadn't expected he would receive one.

The Captain had taken them ashore because he had promised, he said, not to let them out of his sight. He had also exchanged their English money for French so that they could buy the cards to mail home, and souvenirs.

60

"Three francs, fifty centimes." He had counted out the strange, unfamiliar money — three colored paper bills and some small coins.

They paid for the cards and the stamps with the centimes and there was still enough left over to buy two bars of French chocolate. It tasted like chocolate but not like English chocolate.

Buying the gifts hadn't been so easy but Penny had pointed to the little lace handkerchief she wanted for her mother and the lady behind the counter had said, "*Ah, un mouchoir!*" It took a little longer to find the right present for her father: a key ring with a tiny Eiffel Tower hanging from it to prove it had come from France. "*Pour la clé. C'est bon,*" the lady had said.

Maxwell had been very impressed and had bought the same for his mother and father.

After that Penny had bought *une petite poupée* for herself — a little doll dressed in French costume to keep her little Austrian doll company. Maxwell had bought for himself a model of the *Reine de France*.

"And now *deux glaces*, I think," the Captain had said. He had led them to where chairs and tables were set out on

the sidewalk in front of the stores. The two ice creams were
larger than any Penny and Maxwell had ever seen, topped
with real cream and decorated with fresh fruit. For himself

the Captain ordered coffee and chatted to the waiter as easily as if he had been a Frenchman, too.

Cars flashed by on the road in front of them, blowing their horns for no reason at all, and the horns made high, impatient sounds. It was much noisier than in England. Even the policemen joined in, blowing whistles instead of waving the traffic on quietly as they did at home. And everyone drove on the wrong side!

"Wrong for you," the Captain said, "but it's the right side for the Frenchman."

Maxwell saw the white cliffs first and as the *Reine de France* crept closer they grew larger and taller and whiter.

"We're home!" Penny cried. And she knew now just how the boat felt when she blew out the words on her siren: happy to have had such a good trip, but glad to be home again.

"Have you anything to declare?" There was Maxwell's grandfather holding up the card with all the things written on it that you weren't supposed to bring into the country without declaring.

Maxwell and Penny couldn't see model boats mentioned,

nor dolls, nor handkerchiefs, nor key rings — but they declared them just the same, putting them down on the counter for Maxwell's grandfather to see. Very solemnly he marked each piece with a touch of white chalk which meant: These have been declared and are allowed into the country.

"You had us very worried," he said to them afterward. Then he said to Maxwell, "I believed you were old enough and sensible enough to be trusted. Penny was in your charge. You shouldn't have let her out of your sight. I should be angry with you."

"I know," Maxwell said. "I didn't mean it to happen, really I didn't."

"There wasn't anything to worry about," Penny assured Maxwell's grandfather. "Maxwell knew his way around."

"Well, you're back safe and sound and we'll say no more about it. Now, tell me," he asked Penny, "what did you think of it over there?"

Penny thought for a moment. Then she said, as Tom had said, because now she knew exactly what he had meant, "It's the same as here, really — only different."